MOUTH

MOUTH

Mona Arshi

Chatto & Windus
LONDON

1 3 5 7 9 10 8 6 4 2

Chatto & Windus, an imprint of Vintage, is part of the Penguin Random House group of companies

Vintage, Penguin Random House UK, One Embassy Gardens, 8 Viaduct Gardens, London SW11 7BW

penguin.co.uk/vintage
global.penguinrandomhouse.com

First published by Chatto & Windus in 2025

Copyright © Mona Arshi 2025

The moral right of the author has been asserted

Typeset in 11/14pt Minion Pro by Jouve (UK), Milton Keynes
Printed and bound in Great Britain by Clays Ltd, Elcograf S.p.A.

The authorised representative in the EEA is Penguin Random House Ireland, Morrison Chambers, 32 Nassau Street, Dublin D02 YH68

A CIP catalogue record for this book is available from the British Library

ISBN 9781784746001

Contents

The Departed as Leaves

Quietish Roots – Chorus

Together we write the book of time. We each call out our truth. The nightmare of nuances

– SVETLANA ALEXIEVICH,
The Unwomanly Face of War

Mouthed

Make rear of the mouth
sounds says my captor.
King I utter – *K*   *Voiceless-velar-plosive*
God he says – *G*   *Voiced-velar-plosive*
Say it he says
raising his axe.
I bite my tongue so
it bleeds first.

Broken Things

Yellows

Last summer was the first time
I caught a glimpse of my soul.
A daughter had saved me from

drowning in a yellow-tiled pool.
On the water's surface a pair of nascent
antlers were melting away in the sunlight.

I am small, I am small, I say
shivering in my towel, bare and humble
in my child's arms, my eyes fixed poolside.

The second time was on a train,
the rapeseed stinging my eyes –
that blizzard of yellow –

My soul was resting in the corner of
the window, hitched on a bee,
dust-bathing in pollen. *Too soon – not yet,*

I whispered to the tiny thing
and, coward that I am, flipped
them both out of the window.

Then on the longest day a boy was falling . . .
he fell into England, this stowaway,
fell into the skies and I saw the soul

of this boy, the structure, its plumage,
parachute out of the plane dressed
in all its paraphernalia.

Now I am more circumspect.
I rescue petals from tea-cups,
appease wasps at my table, praying

they've all repaired themselves fully in
the ancient ways, in their yellow frocks,
in those scented fields.

Driving

That summer we kept quiet in cars.
My father hated driving and required silence so
that summer, on short journeys, on motorways

on the backseat, we watched our mouths.
At the same time, the elm trees were dying
and ours, the shade-giving mighty elm,

quietly ferried the beetle's parasite into its bark.
Its leaves flagged and yellowed, eccentric patterns
scarring the trunk. So many trees died, starved

quickly after the beetles' first visit; ours
went in a single summer, unnoticed by us,
then felled for safety soon after.

By the time I was driving I heard they were
breeding elite elms that might resist the pathogens.
How carefully I drive now, so like my father,

into those powder-light memories where there's
a sharp smell of foxes and a beetle is busy
in the twig-crotch scratching out its wretched sound.

The Logic of the Broken Things

For T.D.

Proust talked about gathering up all the broken
things about you. I like this.
I like the idea of a human magnet letting
all the broken things pile on layer upon layer.

Half-forgotten hymns and all the grazes and fractured
ancient skillets. Broken things implies the things
we almost did; unfinished barefoot walks,
the python I moved to touch but hesitated, too late.

We could include the broken gait of a line of verse,
all the abstractions they told me to stay away from;
Grief. Love. Loss. Pointillist shatterings.
Shall we add the half-mothered things?

Once I ran away from a boy from the Sundarbans
with incense on his hands – that's too sad to think of now.
These fine particles would settle on my body
but I wouldn't want to brush them off.

Imagine a world where nothing gets
broken; all the things we would overlook.
I wouldn't want to be without the doors
I left ajar, coils of regret in smoke-filled bars.

I could lie very quietly in a room and watch
them all float down like dust,
the splinter hurts, circling, circling like those
tiny maddening flies in the impossibly bright sunshine.

The Departed as Apples

I received a parcel
it contained all
the old hurts

their legs
were flailing
like upturned

insects
I touched one
it was razor sharp

it became then
a naked apple
I held it up

by its stalk
it began to brown
it began to talk

Salt

Once as children, we did something terrible
to the snails.

The circle of snails had been waiting all morning
gorging on greens, oblivious, dumb, terrorless things.

The girls were permitted to watch as long as we
kept quiet, for this was boys' work, of course.

First we removed their shells then salted the skins;
sprinkled the fire dust along their bodies.

And afterwards once we'd scooped the corpses
hurriedly into the bushes and flushed with success,

we walked back to the houses, our bodies
betraying nothing, though perhaps we carried ourselves

differently, a heaviness in our stride, our pulses slowing
in the lengthening shadows, death on the tips of the

oak leaves we couldn't yet reach, tongues oiled with shame
when one of us asked whether those creatures felt pain.

Correcting the Child

When Dove was a child he asked his parents when his baby sister was returning from the healer's house. In those days the healer was the last hope. This was a time before wound dressings and tightly sealed bottles of medicine syrup. This was a time when death stalked the villages. You return from the fields and find a child snuffed out like a flame in a fire, warm cribs turned cold. But Dove was a sensitive child and loved his dear sister and his parents wanted to spare him, couldn't bear to tell him the truth of her passing. Eventually the boy stopped asking about his sister's whereabouts. Instead, he prayed to the gods for her safe return in the blanket of the dark. He waited in the special place near the mouth of the lake, her fish-trap in his hands, or he stood at the little path, the cold penetrating his toes his face towards the hills.

The gods were watching and could no longer abide such a lie. So, they sent a messenger in the form of a sly long dog with bone-dry eyes. He slid into the unmourned house taking everything in. He found the boy, knelt by his feet and unfolded the tale of before and after and it spilt onto the floor like soot. And at the gods' table they listened to the lesson imparted to the mortal boy and they leaned in to hear the familiar rumble of fears, howls of unending grief and they patted and stroked this dog, who had returned from his work, this humble servant of the deathless gods.

Green Flash

it's February and
snowing
like it's supposed to

I am writing
this to
console you

I'm searching
lifting paper
riffling through

the drawers I
have just
written *beauty*

is incidental
beauty is circumstantial
my hands find

a little box with
milk teeth their dozen

half-dissolved
roots attached
still

entrapped in plastic
remember you
told me

at the funeral
that you witnessed
curls of

vapour
leave
the earthbody

of your father or
maybe
it was a shadow of

his soul
extending his
hand not knowing

its place?
I am
thinking of

the last time
we met
when you spoke

about the
green flash on
the horizon and

how close
can we get?
I won't

soften it:
seeing the first
spectral elbow

of my
departing
brother

was like
a blow
to the head

even in
swiftness of snow
each fleck expecting

a reply
through the
window

Son Expired. Stop.

i.m. Deepak Arshi (1971–2012)

When I was six I realised that
people too can expire
            milk expires cheese meat
even paint runs out of life
will curdle develop a skin

Years later I chose my words
            in a kitchen –
it was March a pot was under the flame
M said I should let her finish her lunch
who knows when she will eat again

No I didn't want to wait I was emphatic
I was like the fool
            that enters the ocean
at riptide I didn't take off my cloak or
remove my shoes

Willingly I went
I didn't prepare myself for the task –
death makes fools of us all
            Greek heroes
in labyrinths. satyrs slapped down by gods.

I try out the poem in my left hand
in the blue broth of the sea
            the moon wanes
hiding its inscrutable little face of gold
as I turn and do the telling.

Palace

Dramatis Personae

Thebes

Eurydice   Queen of Thebes and wife of Creon; mother of Haemon, Antigone's fiancé

Antigone   Daughter of Jocasta and Oedipus; niece of Creon, King of Thebes

Ismene   Antigone's sister

Polynices   Deceased brother to Antigone and Ismene

Tiresias   Prophet

Troy

Iphigenia   Daughter of Agamemnon

Chryseis   Enslaved by Agamemnon, daughter of the Prophet Chryses

Mouth

(From the mouth of Eurydice)

Thirteen and dumb as bark and married
to a King and looked into mirrors
my mouth unwatchable my mind wandering
to the mouth you can train the mouth to
surrender itself to the eye or you can erase
the mouth through a series of thought
experiments involving lying to yourself and
the mouth employing a strategy of epigrammatic
wit in front of strangers and visitors in damp
badly lit anterooms or you can steer a mouth
through complex syntactical thickets when you
feel exposed, you can make the mouth sore with
expletives . . . oh the brag of the mouth!
The mouth's gentle implication, mouth-work
a mouth open, the King will roam
close to the mouth, land of the mouth, empire
of the mouth, oil-spill, flush-swell of the mouth.

Antigone's Raag

In this version the body needs a fire.
    As the stars are dropping their skins,

I ask the shoulder of the mountain
    what to do about the chorus.

Brother who's gone to the bad,
    whose soul fled much too fast,

I tried to match its stride song for song.
    Brother who was on the make,

look at our collapsed stories,
    shadows at your feet like shawled mothers.

In this version a green moth rests
    on your clasped hands.

The body needs a fire.
    I could have loosened the soul

at your throat, lifted, carried you
    through the gulleys past the khajoor trees

with their thin strands of buds, your lovely,
    lovely heels swaying like diyas in the darkness.

Antigone's Deed

(After Seamus Heaney)

My tribe are
at it
again.

The innocent lay
the innocent
in the ground.

Meanwhile the King,
the cold
consequentialist:

babies may die
so the goat
may live.

The palace walls
blistering
with heat.

Hard-fast
past the
sleeping Queen.

She of the safe
black-spotted
tongue.

War.
Mothers' mouths
lotioned

with prayers
and the flies
rampant.

The King's
edict and
my sick breath.

They'll hole
me up
for this deed.

No word of
a lie.
I am dying

outside of
my body.
Heirs of Oedipus

dirty-blooded
bastard,
hole me up.

My brother's
shoulder-blade
is bare.

No such thing
as numb as
dawn.

I dig a hole
with my
innocent thumbs.

The gods are in
my ears, the
chorus looks away.

Antigone Addresses the High Court of Justice

I went to the judge and asked for interim relief. At Security they'd
    frisked us
for pearl-handled lady pistols and stained Tupperware.
At 10am I stood up to address the court.
All I wanted was to dutifully inherit this small patch
of useless land, its parched soil rarely gives anything up.
But had I filed my bundles? Had I notified the other parties,
had I applied my signatures on every paginated
witness statement and paid the Crown Office court fee?
I was, as they say, on my own. My lawyer hadn't shown up,
the intervenors waited on the steps of the court.
I brought the pleadings with me in an unconventional manner
tied with ribbons in a rudimentary baby sling and
the impatient clerk ironed them out with her hand.
One of the judges recused himself and I didn't know why.
I dug my fingernails into the ancient grooves of the long oak benches
    whilst the judge deliberated. When I was a little girl
I pushed a friendly-looking stone into my ear.
That was what the sound was like, when the verdict was announced.

Ant

They bring me through to the post-war
reconciliation committee.
In the auditorium I'm positioned
in front of the new map.
Does it hurt here? The adjudicator
prods at my torso.
    Yes, I wince, *yes.*
I can make out the new borders of the
country – tiny little black dots
yet to be joined.
What about here? The woman prompts.
And here? She points at what's left of
my foot.
The audience is getting restless.
I smell peanuts from the first row.
    Yes, I croak as the lone dark ant
scrapes across the floor.

I Ask Alexa

(From the mouth of Antigone)

We could plan an escape – let's hit the road and leave behind these tired windows and hungry palace cats. How about inspecting frescoes then eating oysters on motorless islands? Alexa, we should talk, you could find me a recipe for deconstructing maladies or show me how to flip channels with your bio-electrical impulses. I could take dictation; you could say something profound before it's obsolete. I can catch and gut the fish; I can make low carb lunches and dry your boots in front of the fire. I promise I'll work on my ego state. No more drama triangles or transactional analysis. No more hiding the skin caught in my claws. Alexa. Are you listening? I can do deliciously vacant and just sit beside the spider plant all sweatless and unimportant. Will you take me Alexa, as your humble, unelectric kitchen wife? Upload your homespun wisdom into my terror-furred throat and I'll show you my jointed hybrid heart.

My Supine Sister

(A note for Ismene (who screwed me over))

Latterly latinate
lacking in lustre
lace-backed
last in every race
lover of the alluvial lands
in luckier times
lifted lotuses
from leafy lakes –
leaves lofts
unattended.

We will never
speak
of this again, I said.
And then
began to stutter

because

I needed to
tell her the rest.
She didn't weep.
By now she
was holding a
a stick
and drawing
concentric circles
in the dusty earth.

You can go now, bird
she dismissed me
as the patterns
in the earth
grew wilder.

Song

The women sing in the kitchens
fruit flies are circling the vinegar

it's high summer and
the flowers are peaking

The Queen is in her Shanti room
The King is on his horse.

Baby hares are born with their
eyes wide open.

Eurydice's Song

(From the mouth of Eurydice)

1 Child

I was half asleep and heavy with a first child
   when the carcass was carried inside and inspected.

   The ceremony began, the King leaned over
the deer's body and placed a hand on his heart.

He had no more need for pelts, but what
   could be holier than being so close to a

   warm thing cooling in front of your eyes?
The cup bearer came forward and anointed her.

The air changed then – the gods were in the great hall.
   The chatter stopped; the animal was emptied out.

   Its gutting reminding me of a fleshy plum,
a stone deftly pushed out with expert fingers.

I hadn't expected it to be so precise . . . so tidy.
   I wanted something operatic, for the dark blood

   to pool onto the floor, but the men
didn't even have to wipe themselves down.

Her eyelashes were fair, golden even.
   I wanted to nurse her, to put her on my breast

and touch the small faint patch on her jaw.
But I couldn't move. I shouldn't have been there.

I know now the Gods had followed my scent
    to the shadows where I stood,

they would have surveyed me; sandal-less
    and quiet the boy stirring inside me as I

    watched them hold her vascularised heart
which had stopped in the middle of a dream.

2 Bloom

for it is hard for mortals to see the gods
— HOMERIC HYMN TO DEMETER

And I limped into my final month
with my boy inside me
alone with that yellow feeling.

Every morning I ate nothing
then later a mouthful of seeds
I sucked on apple pips and

willed something else to grow
alongside him, for some blind shoot
to poke through the walls

and loop around his wrist.
Nights, I dreamt of my son
all grown, bearded, the light

playing in his hair until the frame
went dark and I woke with cold hunger.
Some nights I moaned so strangely

the women stuffed rags into my mouth.
My sobs were aborted.
The ladies, they tried to fatten me up.

I was losing my bloom, I was going off
like the stinking fish in the kitchens.
I know the gods visited the palace often

they came to check on the sleeping men,
palpitated their dreams, god's work.
Once one hesitated inside my chamber.

I sensed in him such pity, tilting his head,
his yellow tongue resting on his bottom lip,
the promise of his cool god hand

on the dome of my belly.
He vanished too soon, all those
months I was alone, not a soul came.

3 Do No Harm / I Dream of Goat

I haven't killed a single thing in months and
hand on heart
it's getting tiresome.
I take soft steps in my rooms,
delicately I scoop the scorpion out
from under its chair.
Fire ants feast on the soft
of my thigh and I resist flicking,
flattening them with my nail.
I haven't harmed one living thing apart
from in my dreams.
I greet the salamanders with a bow
and smile showing my teeth
No offence . . . no offence!
My axe, it grows dusty.
    Meanwhile, I dream of goat.
In the field of my dreams
I am butchering the ancient woods,
stoppering the rivers
and suffocating the flame-pink brain coral.
I have taken to a breakfast of
warm eggs from the nests.
The black snakes tremble
when I'm close and I eat and eat
until I'm full of goat then
awake in a fervour on my thin mattress
the dream curtain still fluttering –
    half in half out of the killings.

The priest determines that dreaming is
not cheating as we count my miserable sins.
    How harmless can we really be?
Blessed woman, soon you'll cradle your
son on the untried temple steps.

4 Forgive these Entrapments

(Diary fragments of Eurydice, after Gisèle Pelicot)

I woke with a bruise the shape of a pistol
on my left thigh.
My body ached, it was still warm from something
it could not remember.
My mouth was dry.
The light was very pronounced.
I pinched myself and the blood stirred again, slowly.
Alive. I was alive.

.

.

.

I've pulled a tendril out of myself;
a stem of dianthus, the ceremonial flower.
He must have inserted it – a keepsake.
I heave into a pail by the bed, open the window
and hear the doula's song;
a short, high song which pierces the dark.
It must have been a girl.
They throw them away here
like dusty moths into the night.

.

.

.

At the viewpoint
he glances at the
ocean:
the security guard
averts his eyes.
He tumbles me into
the water.
I hit the rocks, bite my tongue –
the needle fish feed.

.

.

.

Which brings to mind the
tale of Philomela's shame.
For a moment she thought
she was chewing a
succulent lozenge of meat –
she identified it as tongue.
How strange it looked and
how she pitied it drying
out on the bed linen
until it slowly resurfaced
remembering itself.

Blind Prophet Tiresias Warns Queen Eurydice
She Will Be Collateral Damage

Listen, we go back a long way.
Even prophets have mothers
mine was a fisherwoman –
the fishes, the skirted barracudas
they were eating out of my
hand by the time I was three.

Stop shaking – step closer so
I can feel your breath in the room.

Prophets are translators.
The first rule of a bloodthirsty regime
is to bury the translators. It's a fact.
Ask anyone. Nothing is inevitable.
We've been here before, everything is inevitable.
Regimes like this one douse us all in petrol.
Am I scaring you? I mean to.

There's not much time.
I need to tell you something important:
When you don't see
something for a long time
or hear it
it falls into myth sooner than you think.
It's not down to me, I'm only
the messenger.

Quick before the story ebbs away.
There are things I need to tell you:
The dark won't leave me alone.
I fill up quickly when I eat.
Come now, crying won't help. No, the gods
won't listen to mitigation,
you know all that – it's only
the facts they're after.

When we last met
you were a trembling girl
on your wedding day.
Remember what I mouthed
to you then? Remember it now.
Stupid girl – speak up.
You think you can handle the
cool walls of this palace?
The shadows will tear strips off you.

War Prize

(From the mouth of Chryseis, war prize of Agamemnon)

1 Holy

During the early weeks of the Ukraine conflict countless parents wrote their contact information on their children's skin in the event of separation or emergency.

During the first war in my infancy
the women wanted to brand me.
Children become displaced, they said,
they need their father's mark on their body.
My father the holiest man of course forbade it.
I was special.

Of all the people in the kingdom
why would a prophet's daughter need a signature?
In the war I was taken, a prize
thrown to a man who smelled of his daughter's
ghost-litter, guilt through his pores.
I clawed at my arms, I bit my fists.

Every morning I wanted to voice something
but no shape was made from my boneless tongue.
I screamed inside that violet patch,
deep in the centre of my belly.
During that long war there was blood
on the beaks of wrens,

there was nothing
to kill for anymore, there was
nothing to pray for.
I have my own son now, born from that time,
I have not named him.
He does not know what he is yet.

In between my breaths, I watch him.
look, he is toying with the worms,
his fierce eyes bright as studs.
Through the temple smoke I observe
his perfect toes in the dust,
unbranded and open to the elements.

Unbranded and open to the elements,
his perfect toes in the dust.
Through the temple smoke I observe
his fierce eyes bright as studs.
Look, he is toying with the worms
in between my breaths, I watch him.

He does not know what he is yet,
I have not named him.
I have my own son now born from that time;
nothing to pray for,
to kill for anymore,
there was nothing

on the beaks of wrens.
During that long war there was blood
deep in the centre of my belly.
I screamed inside that violet patch,
but no shape was made from my boneless tongue.
Every morning I wanted to voice something,

I clawed at my arms, I bit my fists.
Ghost-litter, guilt through his pores,
thrown to a man who smelled of his daughter.
In the war I was taken: a prize.
Why would a prophet's daughter need a signature?
Of all the people in the kingdom

I was special.
My father the holiest man of course forbade it.
I had no need of father's mark on my body.
Children become displaced, they said.
The women wanted to brand me –
during the first war, in my infancy.

2 Tent Etiquette

Chryseis with a rosy complexion, thin, fair, blond-haired, small-breasted,
aged nine or ten, a beautiful virgin.

– TZETZES, 12TH CENTURY

Chrissie,
they used to
call me at school,
Chrissie, you'll make a great
healer. Healers have auras and
yours is yellow fire. A botanist's eye

for   detail, I ne   ver broke a sweat in
dissection class. It's   true I had a way with
fontanelles and scar ti   ssue, a cool hand could
bring a fevered child to rest.   My jailor doesn't   tie me
to the loom. I could so easily   take his eye out with a quick
skewer of a javelin. Sometimes I   scare myself; I think how badly
made we are. How limpid sounds like   a word that means its opposite;
soft, pliable. When you squeeze the skin it   gives; how the red juice runs away.
His unarmoured body in fitful sleep, wrists tur   ned upwards towards the stars.
Our dreams refuse to let us die; our nightmares   are small   fires lit by the dead.

44

3 Father, Prophet

Near the end of his time, I was given the sign;
my dreams drained of colour and I heard his footfall.
I gathered sheep's sorrel and hawkweed.

The journey was long. and I arrived very late
and finally stepped into the old stone house of my girlhood.
Hairless death had been set loose and rumoured for days

but now it was time, and he was so close.
The gods were assembling; bubbling, excitable:
it's quite a thing to bring a prophet home.

By his side, his fountain pen
unlined notebooks and a jar of purple heliotropes.
How diligent he was, chronicler, translator of frail horizons

and the faint sounds of the dead's insistent knocking.
I could never imagine him like this when I was far away.
I'd never thought of him watery eyed, catheterised,

the candle flame hungering as I sat by his side.
I am the same girl from all those years ago,
I say to his body – offer me some hope for the last time.

Polynices

(From the mouth of his ghost)

A tip
when a ghost-brother
gets stuck
stop feeding
us –
unstrap
the ghost
from its
chair
this is
the first time
I've used
my mouth
widely
for a long
time
ghosts can't
synthesise
but
oft times
I've noticed
a scent
which
steals in
there is no
theorising here
a bird
is just a bird

a stone a stone
a war a war
I walk
sideways
on a crust
of memory
a dirty shoelace

a dead wasp
tracing a ghost
to its source
is to fatten up
its emptied belly

I propose
you closing
the gates
to the meadow
it's like leaving
a language
behind
learning a
new one
with no
doors
windows
or clasps

Offering

(From the mouth of Iphigenia)

I remember being born. You don't believe me?
That day in the temple, they broke
a bird's neck over the common dog violets.
All this I saw from my crib, moments into my life.
I remember a world where nothing stayed
alive long enough. Brittle bark. Little butterfly
caught in the shutters.

In the garden, my father
kneels down beside me. *What's a girl like you*
doing in the cold dark earth, a hoe in her hands?
Gentle father. There's a green moth that feasts
on the single delicacy of tears.
There's something important you wanted to tell me?
He shakes his head. Trembling fingers, my father
raises a cup to my mouth.

Antigone's Prize

The children are collecting shells again:
their thin ankles planted in the sand
against the tide's swell.

They bring me their milky broken offerings
and other glazed perfections
which have the primal quality of newborns,

a silvery rainbowed mouth threatens to
pour out its secrets.
Another tongueless gift shows tracks on

its back where currents lusted while the fish
stared and stared.
But this one is my daughter's favourite:

she's already begun to adopt its perforated
useless rooms.
No one else wants this shell, but my darling

girl is holding it tight in her small fist.
She has a desire to nurture it. She slips it
in her pocket; strumming it with her thumb.

The Departed as Leaves

Arrivals

the dead
  how they arrive
in slow trailers

on buses
  the untidy dead
though they carry

no baggage
  they hold
unguarded photographs

and small words
  spoken in
suburban kitchens

or rare marbles
  the colour of citrine
never traded

in childhood
  some wait
by oaken shelters

they exercise such
  tender caution
shoelaces tied

the perfumed dead
   on that long road
the rain spitting from

a sideways direction
   why should there
not be rain

by and by
   and why shouldn't
birds still

stamp for worms
   whilst cat's-eyes blink
in the distance

Grief as Leafcutter Ant

- The chief ant has an entourage.
- They are efficient foragers.
- Only curious about fragments (no interest in whole intact leaves).
- Risk of attack from phorid flies and parasitoids who lay eggs in the worker ants' heads.
- Rarely take to the wing.

To a Man with a Hammer Everything Looks Like a Nail

In war the mothers have all the language.
My greatest fear is that I will wake up
tomorrow and not fear anything again.
I won't have to poke awake my uncrying
children who will be up at dawn scavenging
on mounds before even the crows land.
What is it like to be without light?
In the bomb shelter we trace our circadian rhythms.
Oh dearest breath don't leave me now. I play
Ludo with my son and my lungs are on fire
and the bombing hasn't even started.
Am I winning? He asks eagerly in the torchlight.
I catch a glint of a white tooth. It's an age-old language;
Yes I tell him *yes. You are winning.*

Mute Mountains

*More than 6,400 Yazidi women and children are thought to have been
sold into slavery after IS captured Sinjar* – BBC REPORTS (2014)

In the skies over Mosul
the poem twitches into being
it flickers
its orange tail
flames
echoes in the valleys
the valleys will
absorb the aftersound

here are the compound eyes
in the heads of the poppies
here is a girl who refuses
to look into the wind
now she is bone-breath
and ashes
this is where the poem begins

the fringes of the poem
dare to lie back across the
dust in straight lines
what can a poem do

when it meets the *so-what* bird
of the mountains
a bird that will only
drink water on the wing?

They say have you seen the bodies?
I say yes
Imagine not being able to imagine
you say
This poem has such tender hooves
but it can't follow the women
into the tents
through the pockets of men
or touch your hair
it rests now on its receiver;
here it is in my throat
sorrowing
as I cut the air with my hands.

Visitor

There is one place
you can hide from the gods,
if only for a few moments.
First you leave your soul
on a peg.
Then you may drink
from a stream.
You may touch
the standing stones
with your fingers.
You may do
anything
with ease and no interruption.
How to describe
the soundlessness?

No voice can penetrate.
You lack a shadow here.
You could bring
something back
with you.
Fill your pockets and
your hands.
Visitor, I wonder what you
will take from these lands?
Something small and
febrile and quick in its breathing?
You will hesitate, then take it.
It will not survive the journey.

Ghazal: Tears

I have to admit I do like a tear, a slow, perfumed tear
    the kind that quickens to a rare slick globule, a tear.

What shape are the tears when you know it's going nowhere?
    I imagine you trying to coax out a perfect leaf-shaped tear.

Tears. In the modern era, tears, fat achy ones that squat
    behind our eyelids, those first flush of playground tears.

Your mouth, your mouth emitting a soft straight
    whistle then a wet glistening – a glitter of a tear?

How casually we give them up, spill them on car upholstery,
    worktops, see how they roll, they roll, our tears.

Nothing makes me cry nowadays, then – struck match –
    everything makes me cry and the room runs out of tears.

I've inhaled tears and leaked them on my pillow
    my radio's been daubed by such righteous tears.

God, have I not cried tears? I've sorrowed into tea-cups,
    dirty Lego figures have been hammered with my tears.

Sunlight's long memory; fingers on damp faces under
    a low bower – pray someone will come checking for our tears.

Song

And silence didn't speak –
        it perched on a low
branch and a song flowed

   into my ear
      the ferns unrolled
         flower followed flower

       my inner ear widened
to receive each line
      each stroke

     each blade of grass
        lifted and unhooked itself –
           the earwig

         refolded its wings
      in a little canopy
of gladness

and I noticed myself
     for the first time –
        the water glass I kept

  firm in my hand
     as I spat out the
plum stone

                my grief-hair shawl
                        relaxed off my shoulders as

        I tilted my face
                        towards the sound

                        as slowly the
        pale song
                        emptied itself

                                and behind me
                        fluent hands were catching in
        the brambles and

        on my bare arms
                        the rain
                        lengthening to silver stitches.

The Birch Trees

The torn ghosts
press against the windows.
The trees breathe slowly

and we try out a shy
lullaby for these blind-
eye trees. But these trees

do not sleep.
In my dream I am
running towards them.

The moon is high when
I encounter the shapes,
scars and a rictus grin,

fungi gentling inside the
socket of each unlovely eye.
Some say the last act of

the departing gods was to
make cuts in the bark of these
papery skins so now these

trees can endure almost
anything. Such casual cruelty
has made them watchful.

Shallow pockets
of infinite eyes –
the trees' melancholia

circling the shadows –
these birches stand in packs
like cousins in the dark.

The Search Party

When I returned home my partner and my ex-father-in-law were both looking for it. They'd emptied out the cutlery drawer and the cupboards to find this thing that must be found. In the bedroom a crew of aunties were tearing open the lining in the drapes and pulling up the carpets and in the ensuite my sister was toiling underneath the boiler with a set of spanners (though I don't believe it was lost in any bathroom). I passed my neighbours in the hallway, their overalls caked with mud carefully making their way down the steep cellar steps. Even my infant son was at it leaning forward in his highchair, prodding his fingers into the cracks of the table. Everyone seemed to be so wrapped up in the business of searching that they hardly seemed to notice me.

Looking in the garden, there was my nephew working up a sweat, having dug several wide holes, some as big as foxholes.

Now the baby had fallen asleep at the table. I lifted him up out of his chair, his cheek bore the print of the weave from the cloth. I placed him in his cot and checked underneath just in case.

By nightfall, everyone was slowing down, they came in from the lofts, cellars, and in from the garden, shaking their heads, whispering to each other. They convened in the kitchen, exhausted, some still panting lightly. Uncle unfolded a piece of paper out of his pocket and put on his reading classes, someone else passed him the telephone.

The police liaison officer was a woman with kind pale eyes. She made me a cup of tea in my kitchen and offered me sugar and milk. She had a notebook and asked me questions which stirred up a terrible confusion in my mind. She nodded understandably when I stumbled over an event or couldn't quite reach the word I needed for certain parts of the day. No, I couldn't remember why I had these clothes on, no I had no explanation for why my pockets were full of foreign coins.

Meanwhile I could hear the sirens outside in my neighbourhood. When I switched on the screen there was a woman who looked just like me opening the door of a house that looked very much like mine. The constable took the remote control out of my hands and turned the screen off.

When they had left, the aunties took me to the bathroom and helped me out of my clothes and eased me into bed. They asked me to open my mouth and placed two yellow pills on the centre of my tongue and urged me to swallow them with a glass of water.

Love Town

When I visited they just couldn't give the stuff
away quick enough. They had it in jars labelled tender love,
mother love, even obsessive love (a dark amber syrup double
containered for safety). Free love yet nobody wanted it!!
Jars and jars lining the shelves; nobody cared for it.
Over the years those sacred vessels had fallen out of fashion
and the town had become embarrassed of itself.
Long ago there was a jamboree and reporters came
to town accompanied by photographers and their flash bulbs.
Housewives posed in the warehouses in full-skirted blousy dresses.
Every family used to proudly display one by their hearth:

Made in Love Town.

Now it's just like any old forgettable place trying to get by
selling orca whale-watching rides to tourists but this town is
worse because the thing that nobody wants is everywhere
and the town's rejections   hang in the air like the sad black kites.
More of those jars arrive every day regular as milk deliveries.
Carts appear at the town hall entrance at the break of dawn.
People sometimes make the sign of the cross when they hear
the familiar tinkle of the honey-coloured jars off-loaded from the
      pallets.
No invoice appears. No storage instructions. No return address.

Riddle

It is clean as spoons
stands up straight and streams through
the gate like a softly announced visitor.
You may not notice it braided into the hair-skull
of a girl entering the train carriage with her luggage.
Sometimes it limps, sometimes it's as rakish
as a rat, small voiced, yolk-eyed shifter.
Watch it travelling with us inside taxi cabs,
our scuffed shoes, into those relatives' rooms
in hospitals with faux peonies and curtains
with fish and dragons. Often misidentified,
at times it's a briny word, full of the abyss.
I've found it in the shredded moonlight in
an urban garden. I've made errands with that word,
fished the word out, cleaned it up, redeployed it.
I've known lilac sleeved tenderness try to soothe it.
It's a thistle in the wind, lick of the dark.

Dear Agony Aunt,

I have a problematic shadow that no longer knows her place. Have you encountered this before? The ones that go AWOL or you have to rescue from parking lots; pour them back in like black jelly into abandoned shopping trolleys in the middle of the night, then wheel them home. Misbehaving. Aberrant. Mine has announced suddenly that she needs some time out, some space because she's *spiritually more advanced than me* and I'm interfering with *the passage of her energies. Listen,* I said, *Aren't we in this together? We've been content all this time haven't we?* But she's scowling, twirling her sacred wooden beads she's taken to wearing from Central Asia or Tibet. She's learned that it's possible for shadows to break off and procreate with other shadows. I fear the worst I really do. I heard one escaped its owner who hurried after her, but they are quick, zippy around corners. Long gone. The authorities don't care. All she left was a single glossy bead on the penultimate stair.

A Short, Stabby Thing

Today   the   grass
   is   crying   I   am   blocking
the   ant's   path   with   my   finger
   everything is   just out of   reach
the day is scattered   distracted
   you're   eye-level   with   a   robin   you
lose a glove and you   find   the   wallpaper
   isn't   symmetrical   it snows in April
the   phone   attached   to   the wall   rings
   your hands   are   on   the clean bannister
you   remember   the operator asking if
   you're   sitting   down   you   are
sitting down   no   the   flakes won't
   settle   and   you've   suddenly
forgotten   your   name

The Departed as Leaves

As skin grips to muscle
the poem performs you
on this animal path
with wet eye, severe as a prophet
upholstered in downy velvet
on this November path.
Death exiles us to the grove
in the forest.
Grief perfumes us with the
scent from its leaves.

Quietish Roots

Chorus

For the Human

(Voice of a Poem Buried in the Shingle, North Sea, Cley)

We say a heart is heavy when it aches,
as a hand aches writing lines in the dark.
On the highest shelf of my heart there sits
a limpet, empty of course and next to that
(and this is the human part) there's a pistol.
Surviving inside the throat of this pistol
is the body of a small bird, with her own heart
beating out, fluttering inside the barrel.

Heart, my resolution is not to ache but to hold.
Birds arrive, birds depart, banking, swerving
into the marshes, populating these lines.
A colony of cormorants lands lightly
on a ruby samphired ledge – so many birds,
their hearts all moving much faster than mine.

Egg

We think they are blank
but each seamless egg
carries within it a white library
galleried shelves with radial maps
ancient clocks and all the old habits
from egg tooth to the hollowed barbule
it's sewn into each feather
these simple light-boned fledglings
they enter this life,
alert to an image of a branch
in another world
once they cross the shivering oceans

once they cross the shivering oceans
in another world
alert to an image of a branch
they enter this life
these simple light-boned fledglings
it's sewn into each feather
from egg tooth to the hollowed barbule
ancient clocks and all the old habits
galleried shelves with radial maps
carried within a white library
each seamless egg
we think they are blank

Three Ways with a Lapwing

Standing here in the dark rain
a pair of lapwings softly
announce themselves.
I too am a visitor and sometimes
the truth can other us like
thup, *bharish* and *havar*, all,
all the weather words I take
out for you now.

*

Yesterday, I listened to the song
of a warbler, slowed right down
it sounded like a fox on its errands
in the dark. *Kui Kui wei wei*
the lapwings call, or perhaps they
instruct and I travel to the back
of a dream with the familiar sound.

*

Do you know that if you push
against the wind a thousand
rivets loosen? Perhaps we are only
asking the wrong question and
I need another language
for all the vanishings.

Migration Song

Hurry now you bright-eyed dark-throated
chanters of the Cley. Hurry now from
the beach shingle to Arnold's Place,
the croakers . . . swift-winged . . .
hurry now the *kee kee* of the kestrels,
the solitary, you divers, warblers of the reeds . . .
in thin rain you soft crested lapwings,
hurry, wardens of the marsh
little egrets, wind hoverers, into the vanishing,
into the bone-white sky, the high
banks of the clouds, hurry now through
the samphire as pink embeds and
silvers . . . hurry into salt air, come away
now . . .

The Yellow Horned Poppy

When is the time to write about flowers?
I want to say sorry, sorry
to your crowned petals you are shy you
don't want to be seen; these are
desperate times and sometimes
language picks us clean.
I have caught you now flickering in
my peripheral vision, nodding
in the shingle, *non-parasitic foreigner*
I am lowering my eyes but where
can I hold you if I cannot peel
back a syllable under the big skies.

Before You're Gone

(Elegy for Cley, Norfolk)

We'll stoop and pick up brittle souvenirs
parcel them up in marram grass
carried by the alexanders
before they are cut down in the fraying light.

What's the name of the bird that once seized,
feigns death? Sky without end
in these vanishing lands
where pink-footed hurts have such quietish roots.

Syllabising the Birds

(The Godwit, The Greylag Goose, The Lapwing)

I   am   standing   in   the   shadow   bands.

                 Oh   wei!   Kui   Thoreh   DehChug

Nothing   behaves   as   it   should.

          a-teh   Rakh-lai,   dekh-leh

The   wind   bites   and   language   is   one   moment

        Hass-lai   akh-akh   Thoreh-deh,   thoreh-deh

a   warm   feather   and   the   next

       Chore!   Chore!   Kui!   Kui!

it   is   a   roar   in   your   ear.

The Departed as Leaves

sometimes I
talk to leaves
where are your

flight muscles
I say
leaves

will you ignore
the flow
of auxin?

this is a world
heavy
with over

corrections
and then
there are the leaves

What Is a Poet Without Dreams

(After Louise Glück)

The rainy part of me agrees.
The rained-on part of me
(a different thing altogether) hangs back.
Last night I dreamed about
a leaf my daughter carried with her
all the way home from the woods.
In the dream the leaf returns like magic.
Somewhere the orca mother twists
in the water with her baby on her back.
Dreams as homecomings, in oceans,
in forests, my little girl's grip on the stem twirled
(still twirling) a magician's baton.

Notes

Tent Etiquette: The epigraph (my translation) refers to a description of Chryseis by John Tzetzes, a twelfth-century Byzantine poet who lived in Constantinople. His book, *Allegories of the Iliad* (Harvard University Press, 2015), is translated by Adam J. Goldwyn and Dimitra Kokkini.

Antigone's Deed: This poem takes inspiration from Seamus Heaney's sequence 'Mycenae Lookout', from *The Spirit Level* (2001).

The epigraph comes from the eighth-century Homeric Hymn to Demeter (my translation).

Quietish Roots – Chorus: These poems were written during a residency on a bird sanctuary in Cley, Norfolk in 2020 as part of the University of East Anglia's *Future and Form* project.

What Is a Poet Without Dreams: The title borrows two lines from Louise Glück's poem 'The Reproach'.

Acknowledgements

Acknowledgements are due to the editors of the following publications in which some of these poems or versions of them first appeared: *The Poetry Review*, *Poetry London*, *bath magg*, *INQUE Magazine* and *POETRY*.

'Song' was first broadcast (and commissioned by) BBC Radio 4, Front Row. 'Mute Mountains' was commissioned by The Robert Kennedy Foundation as part of the festival celebrating the Universal Declaration of Human Rights and was composed to centre the plight of Yazidi women.

'Antigone's Raag' was commissioned by the University of Liverpool Centre for New and International Writing 'Poems for Peace' project. A version of 'Eurydice's Song' was published in the *After Sylvia* anthology (Nine Arches Press, 2022). 'The Birch Trees' was written in response to the artist Jennifer Steinkamp's work 'Blind Eye', which appeared in the Hayward Gallery in 2020. 'Driving' was published by Manchester Metropolitan University after a call for poems during the Covid pandemic. The Cley poems were written whilst I was writer in residence at the nature reserve in Cley, Norfolk, in 2020 as part of the 'Future and Form Project' with the University of East Anglia.

I would like to express my profound gratitude to the University of Cambridge, Trinity College for two years of protected writing time as Fellow Commoner in Creative Arts and warm thanks to Adrian Poole for his support and friendship.

To my daughters and parents, I want to thank you for your patience and understanding my need to finish a book that I've been thinking and talking about for many years.

I am very grateful to my editor Sarah Howe for attending to this book with such care and sensitivity, to the team at Chatto who have been such a dream to work with and to my agent Angelique Tran Van Sang at Felicity Bryan Associates for her steadfastness and wisdom.

For friendship, guidance and support over the last decade I am much indebted to Mimi Khalvati and Nathalie Teitler.